better together*

* This book is best read together, grownup and kid.

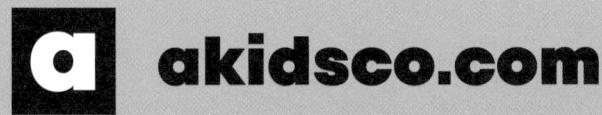 akidsco.com

a
kids
book
about

a kids book about SUSTAIN-ABILITY

by Amber Troutman

A Kids Co.
Editor Emma Wolf
Designer Rick DeLucco
Creative Director Rick DeLucco
Studio Manager Kenya Feldes
Sales Director Melanie Wilkins
Head of Books Jennifer Goldstein
CEO and Founder Jelani Memory

DK
Delhi Technical Team Bimlesh Tiwary Pushpak Tyagi, Rakesh Kumar
Senior Production Editor Jennifer Murray
Senior Production Controller Louise Minihane
Senior Acquisitions Editor Katy Flint
Acquisitions Project Editor Sara Forster
Managing Art Editor Vicky Short
Managing Director, Licensing Mark Searle

First American edition, 2025
Published in the United States by DK Publishing, 1745 Broadway, 20th Floor,
New York, NY 10019

First published in Great Britain in 2025 by
Dorling Kindersley Limited, 20 Vauxhall Bridge Road, London SW1V 2SA
A Penguin Random House Company

The authorised representative in the EEA is
Dorling Kindersley Verlag GmbH. Arnulfstr. 124, 80636 Munich, Germany

A catalog record for this book is available from the Library of Congress.
A CIP catalogue record for this book is available from the British Library.
ISBN: 978-0-2417-4348-5

DK books are available at special discounts when purchased in bulk for sales
promotions, premiums, fund-raising, or education use. For details, contact:
DK Publishing Special Markets, 1745 Broadway, 20th Floor, New York, NY 10019
SpecialSales@dk.com

Printed and bound in China
www.dk.com
akidsco.com

MIX
Paper | Supporting
responsible forestry
FSC™ C018179

This book was made with Forest
Stewardship Council™ certified
paper – one small step in DK's
commitment to a sustainable future.
Learn more at www.dk.com/uk/
information/sustainability

For my Mini & Lou.
I love you forever days.

This book supports organizations dedicated to sustainability and climate solutions for a cooler planet.

Intro
for grownups

What do you want most for the kids in your life? Ultimately, many of us just want them to thrive in an unpredictable world. And they need a healthy, habitable planet to make that happen.

Sustainability is more than conservation and protecting endangered species. It's at the root of healing armed conflicts, curbing climate disasters, and mitigating health risks, all of which have outsized impact on the most vulnerable people. At its core, living sustainably means sharing and caring—those elementary values we teach kids from the very beginning.

For some, the topic of sustainability elicits an immediate eye roll or shudder of guilt. After all, we were born into a fossil-fueled culture of consumption that we didn't choose. But we can collaborate to leave things better than we found them, and if you're reading this book, chances are you're already on the right track.

8,066,2

00,925*

*Don't worry about remembering that exact number—it has already changed!

Here's what that looks like spelled out:

EIGHT BILLION
SIXTY-SIX MILLION
TWO HUNDRED THOUSAND
NINE HUNDRED
TWENTY-FIVE.

That's a **HUGE** number.

And do you know what it represents?

THE
NUMBER
OF PEOPLE
ON THIS
PLANET.

And do you want to know something else?

While you were reading that number,
IT JUST KEPT GROWING.

Bigger and

BIG

Ger.

Every. Second.

WILD, right?

Eight billion people means
A LOT of mouths to feed, bodies
to clothe, and thirst to quench.

And our beautiful planet
provides it ALL:

THE FOOD WE EAT,
THE WATER WE DRINK,
THE TREES WE CLIMB,
THE OCEANS WE SWIM IN,
EVEN THE AIR WE BREATHE!

Earth gives us all of it.*

*Plus materials to make our homes, cars, toys, and pretty much everything else!

That must take some serious work, don't you think?

AND HUMANS...

don't always help.

Actually, if we aren't intentional,
we can really mess these
beautiful things up.

That's why we need to have a little chat about...

SUSTAIN

ABILITY.

say what now?

Yeah, that loooooong word is one we all need to know if we want to keep the planet healthy for ourselves and for all the people who come after us.

Sustainability means...

LIVING IN a WAY THAT DOESN'T HARM THE EARTH OR USE UP TOO MUCH OF WHAT OUR PLANET GIVES US.

It's not always clear the damage all our living does to the world around us.

Usually, we don't see the dirty fumes that cars and planes and buildings spit into the air.

Or how plastic from things like grocery bags and packaging piles up in the ocean.

Most of us will never know people who have to leave their homes when forests are cut down.

And we may never set eyes on the massive dumps of old clothes and TVs that swamp disadvantaged communities.

All of this combined can make people and animals sick while also leaving less for those who need the most.

It's important to know these icky side effects are NOT your fault!

BUT, each of us can do something about it.

We can all help our families, friends, and communities make choices that are kinder to the Earth and everything living on it.

But how?, you might ask.

GREAT QUESTION!

I'll answer it with a
few questions for you.

Have you ever transformed an old box into a rocket ship or castle?

Or worn clothes that were passed on from someone else?

Do you have a garden that grows vegetables to eat?

If you answered yes to any
of those questions, then you're
already on your way!

Because sustainability is about getting creative with what you already have, only using what you need, and borrowing from the Earth in a way that allows it to replenish itself.

And there are SO MANY things you and your family can do, big and small.

like...

- Walk, bike, or cartwheel to your favorite places when you can (extra credit for cartwheeling).

- Bring your own bags, water bottles, and utensils when you'll need them, instead of using throwaway plastic.

- Trade toys with your friends when you get bored of them.

- Eat less meat (trust me, a good veggie sandwich beats bologna any day).

- Borrow books from the library.

- Find and shop at a farmer's market, or a store where you can refill your own containers (they do exist!).

- Reconnect with the earth by going for a hike or swimming in a lake.

- Shop for secondhand clothes, furniture, books—basically anything and everything.

- Donate things you don't use anymore.

- Patch the holes in your pants (yeah, that one right there) and other clothing instead of buying something new.

- Eat the leftovers in your fridge so the food doesn't go to waste.

- Help plant a tree—they're good for cooling, for climbing, for flood control, and even for cleaning the air!

Sustainability takes
a dash of creativity,
a dose of empathy,
and a dollop of change.

And it's not all on you—we all have to start somewhere, and it's OK to start small.

You might make mistakes,
and that's OK too.

We all do!

I'm just one of those billions
of ordinary people who populate
this wild and miraculous planet.

And unless you're an alien who beamed this book to outer space, SO ARE YOU.

That means we all have the chance to work together to take care of our shared home.

If you're like me,
you might be thinking,

"WILL ANY OF THE LITTLE THINGS I DO MAKE A DIFFERENCE?"

I Hear you.

LOUD AND CLEAR.

But imagine if all

8,066,2

00,925

of us worked together.

Maybe the changes we make will grow into a HUGE wave of sustainability.

SO LET'S GET TO IT!

AND LET'S DO
IT TOGETHER.

Outro
for grownups

Time to pack your reusable bags and get ready to go! Now's your chance to brainstorm how you can keep living more sustainably. It could be as simple as trying a new plant-based recipe or collecting shower water to use on household plants. Maybe it means sunset walks to pick up garbage in a park or donating items to a local shelter. If you have older kids, they might enjoy transforming secondhand clothing into a new wardrobe (that was my favorite as a teen), or they could help research a solar co-op. It's up to you!

Sustainability doesn't have to feel like a chore. Get creative, channel some generosity, and maybe even have some fun while you're at it. It's all about doing what you can with what you have wherever you are. And whatever works for you and your family counts toward a healthier planet and kinder world.

About The Author

Amber (she/her) wrote this book to invite kids and their grownups into deeper conversations about sustainability. When numerous wildfires devastated cities near her home in Northern California, plumes of smoke arrived on her doorstep, triggering asthma attacks, trapping kids indoors, and casting an apocalyptic orange glow over the region. In the aftermath, securing a healthy planet for all kids, now and in the future, became even more urgent.

While activism and innovation are vital, Amber believes that the small, collective acts of ordinary people can be agents of sweeping change. And with their infectious curiosity and knack for audacity, she trusts that kids have the capacity to hold grownups accountable to their highest ideals. Her hope is that readers will feel empowered to join forces in making more intentional, sustainable choices in their lives.

 @_biglittlebookclub_   🌐 ambertroutman.com

Made to empower.

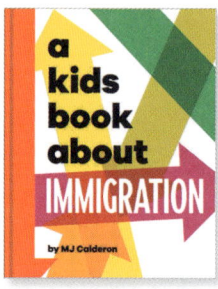

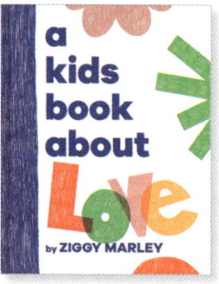

Discover more at akidsco.com